MARGIE

Elizabeth Allen

MARGIE

E. P. DUTTON & CO., INC.   NEW YORK

Margie was previously published in somewhat different
form in *Redbook* under the title "A Dancer in the Dark."

Published simultaneously in Canada by
Clarke, Irwin & Company Limited, Toronto and Vancouver
Library of Congress Catalog Card Number: 69-20015
C64275/76

For J.B., *no stranger*

MARGIE

"Margie!" my father said.

"What have I done now?" I asked.

"Nothing. That's just the trouble." Then, his voice softening, he added, "Perhaps graduate school is not the place for you."

"But Margie's got to do *something*," said my mother, trying not to frown.

We were sitting in the glassed-in back porch behind the kitchen. Before us were hot muffins, bacon, scrambled eggs, and homemade preserves; my father said every day that it was a sin and a shame to eat so well, because we were in the depths of a Depression and there were people who did not have enough food.

I helped myself to another muffin. I didn't see any reason not to eat it, as long as it was there. But what I was thinking was: *It is all over.* For years—because we lived in a college town—I had gone to picnics and tea dances and house parties. But now most of the boys I'd known had graduated, and there was no one left to take me to a party.

"People are being evicted from their homes in Detroit," said my father. "And here we sit . . ." He paused.

"Abby and I made the preserves." My mother always knew what my father was thinking. "They didn't cost much. And you can't stop Abby from making muffins. I know. I've tried. Eat them up, Margie, you're much too thin."

I was encouraged by my mother's remark

that I was too thin. I wanted to be thin; you could not be slinky unless you were thin.

Abby's radio, which had more static than any electrical device I have ever heard, squawked loudly in the kitchen. It was playing a song about dancing in the dark, a favorite of Abby's; she turned up the sound. My father flinched. The radio squawked again, and then stopped dead; fortunately for my father, it went dead often.

"Maybe someone will ask you to Winter Prom yet," Mother said.

"Winter *Prom*—" sputtered my father. "There is no more sense in having that party now, with all the fuss and feathers and corsages—"

"It isn't really a question of one prom," I said, and paused, rather uncertainly. I had not been getting along very well with my father. Actually, I had not been getting along very well with anyone in my family; everyone, including my brother, kept saying "Margie!" and bawling me out.

"They won't let you wear a corsage any more at a prom, Daddy," I went on, for the sake of argument. "They're trying to cut down on the expenses of those big parties."

"Commendable, commendable." My father was frowning down at his plate. "Of course, that's hard on the local florists, and they're having trouble enough as it is."

Nothing seemed to please my father any more. This was a typical example; he couldn't be happy about a prom being dulled by outlawing corsages, because that might put a florist out of business. My mother kept telling me that he was worried about "Conditions" and that, as a sociologist, he was very upset, and that I should please understand. But I was getting tired of understanding.

"Bud's already left for work," my mother said now, to change the subject. "They wanted him early at Kroger's, this morning. He'll just have time to make his ten o'clock class." Then she closed her lips with a worried look. In her haste to guide the conversation, she had chosen an unfortunate topic.

"Bud's working at *Kroger's!*" My father looked really horrified. "Some man with a family may need that job—he's taking bread out of someone's mouth!"

"Now, you look here." My mother, although she kept telling me to try to understand about my father, occasionally sputtered at him herself. "Bud got that job on his own. He turned one down at Registration, and he could have gotten one with Buildings and Grounds, but he was afraid you'd think he used pull because of you and so he got a job off campus."

"The lucky bum," I said. Bud was barely older than I, but he could always get a job and always had money, and I could never get a job and never had money.

"I believe in students earning part of their expenses; you know that . . ." My father looked almost stricken, and this was so unusual that I felt a hot stab of sympathy for him.

"Aren't things getting better now, with Roosevelt and the N.R.A.?" I asked him.

"Yes." My father nodded vigorously. "A great deal has been accomplished. Roosevelt—"

And he was off. My father was a great believer in the New Deal.

"He's setting class against class," said a somber voice. Abby, an apron tied over her neat wine-colored Stylish Stout, came in with the coffee pot and sat down. Abby did not agree with my father about Roosevelt, and often argued with him. Abby was not really a cook; she was a teacher from the Upper Peninsula who was out of work ("I'm out of everything," she had told my mother), and she was on campus finishing a dissertation on Richard Sheridan.

"Abby," Mother said pleadingly. (My mother had told me that five dollars a week was little enough to pay someone to cook all the meals but that she did wish Abby would agree with my father just once in a while.)

The phone rang. It was for me; Pinky Carlin was asking me to go to a party at the Alp House with him.

I could hear my own breath draw in as I listened. I don't know what I'd thought the call might be; not an invitation for Winter Prom, surely. It was just a date for that night. In the old days I would never have accepted a date for Friday night on a Friday morning—I was mortified if I was not dated up for the weekend by Wednesday—and I would not have gone out with Pinky Carlin, either.

"Why, yes," I said. "I'd love to."

"Pinky Carlin?" my mother asked, going by me as I hung up. I could never understand how she could know everything that went on as soon as I did. "Isn't it about time that boy graduated, or went crazy, or something?"

My mother was beginning to show the strain of all the placating she had to do.

"*Mother,*" I said indignantly. I hoped she didn't know that Pinky had never really been registered for any classes. He simply arrived in town every fall, rented an apartment, and went to all the football games and bull sessions and parties. I often wondered if Pinky's own mother did not wonder just when he was going to graduate, or do *something*.

At least I had a date. I felt a little more cheerful; I went up to my room, humming, and got my books. I jammed on the green knit beret that went with my bouclé dress (Mother had knit the dress and Abby the beret. "I got this yarn out of a wastebasket!" she had told me in horror. Abby was always going through wastebaskets). I went downstairs, still humming, and put on my muskrat coat and my fur-trimmed galoshes.

My father was watching me.

"I'd give you a ride, but I'm working right here on my Revision for a while," he said. "I don't have anything on campus until my eleven o'clock."

"I don't mind walking." I was busy with my galoshes.

He was still watching me, and he held up a copy of the *Free Press*. There was a picture of men lined up at a soup kitchen, as well as a picture of a dispossessed family sitting sadly on a street corner among their furniture, and a picture of a dust-bowl farmer, his ruined farm blowing around him.

I nodded.

I told him good-bye and went out the door, and for once I tried conscientiously to think about that black-and-white blur: Conditions. Things are really terrible, I told myself severely.

It was very cold. My breath was pinched back into my nostrils as I walked along. Cold. Winter. Winter; and I didn't have a chance of getting to the Prom, not a chance.

It was colder than it had ever been. The sky was an unpolished gray; the snow was iron beneath me; small flakes pecked at my face.

A gray squirrel coat and a smudge of felt hat lunged ahead of me. It was Tintern Witherspoon, another town girl. She returned my "Hi" with a blurred "Hello," but I knew from experience that Tintern (or Tin Pan, as she was inevitably called) did not want to walk to campus with me. Tintern never walked with anybody. She has no part in this chronicle, and I mention her in passing, only to show that it takes a faculty family to tack a name like "Tintern" onto "Witherspoon."

"Absolutely foul day."

A fur coat similar to mine had drawn up beside me. It was Charla Meadows.

Charla was also a town girl and in fact a neighbor, and we were both daughters of professors, but Charla did not in the least resemble Tintern Witherspoon. Technically, Charla and I were friends. We had gone to the Laboratory School and high school together; we had been in the same sorority; and we had gone to the same parties; but for some reason I had never really been in tune with Charla.

"Cold," she said, not waiting for a greeting. "Absolutely hate it."

"Yes, it's—"

"And it's perfectly *ridiculous* that the Auto Ban applies to graduate students so that I can't drive. *Hate* it."

Charla did not look as though she could hate anything. Good-looking—she'd been the best-looking girl in our high school class except Nan Perry, who was beautiful—she had white skin and dark hair, and even a wind reddening her nose did not coarsen or change her.

"Winter Prom is next week," she went on, gloomily.

"Yes. But of course, when you're in the graduate school . . ." I paused. It made absolutely no difference, when you were in the graduate school. "I mean," I said, "I've gone to enough Winter Proms."

This was an out-and-out lie. I couldn't imagine going to enough Winter Proms.

"They're having Hal Kemp."

I knew perfectly well they were having Hal Kemp.

"Of course, I couldn't get ready for it now anyway," said Charla. "I don't have a hair appointment and I'm not sure about my shoes. . . . I have to have everything just exactly right or it's no good. But I do have my leopard-skin coat, now. I wouldn't have to wear *this* filthy thing. And I'm more or less saving my new white satin. I'm darned if I'm going to wear it to that rat race tonight at the Alp House."

So she was going to the Alp House too. I would undoubtedly see her at Pinky's; Pinky always gave a party before the Alp party.

"Who are you going with?" I asked.

"Morrie," she said. "He called me over a week ago. He's all through Mock Court, and of course even though he's in law school now he gets a bid to everything, he was such a B.M.O.C. —Look." Charla grabbed my arm. "That boy in the dark-blue overcoat is staring at you."

"Oh, Charla, he is *not*." Charla always thought boys were staring.

"He is, but if it doesn't worry you it doesn't worry me." She paused, detaining me before she left for her class at Romance Languages. "I'll probably see you at Pinky's tonight, won't I?" she asked.

"Yes," I said. I felt depressed. I did not really want to go to Pinky's.

"Now, for heaven's sakes, don't take one of Pinky's terrible drinks," Charla told me. "Have tomato juice, along with me."

The trouble was that it hurt Pinky's feelings when you didn't accept one of his drinks, which he carefully put in the correct glasses, with an olive in the one supposed to have an olive in it, and a cherry in the one supposed to have a cherry.

No one knew where Pinky got the ingredients for his drinks. The most anybody else could seem to get hold of was a bottle of bootleg whisky or, occasionally, gin, and except at parties you settled for three-point beer.

"And watch out for Pinky," Charla continued. "He can be terrible when he's had too much. —Although of course," she added, "Pinky's All Right."

I nodded and went off toward U Hall, relieved to be rid of her. My feelings toward Charla had something to do with the people Charla considered All Right. This list was a curious one: Morrie Cohan, a first-year law student, was All Right (he had been a very big man on campus); but had Morrie belonged to a Jewish fraternity, he would not have been All Right. Pinky was All Right because of his parties. Boys who had been on The Team were All Right unless their last names ended in "ski," and practically anyone whose father was on the faculty was All Right, because that was—well, that was All Right.

Ahead of me were a group of girls who were obviously undergraduate.

"If they've dyed those slippers deeper red than my ruby velvet I'm going to kill them," a voice said serenely, and still another wailed that she'd taken a date for the Beaux Arts Ball and it was on the same night as the damn Winter Prom, what did you do about *that,* but at least she could chop up her silver tulle for a costume, she'd been dying to chop up her silver tulle.

I had never even heard of the Beaux Arts Ball. It was apparently a new party. I left them, deliberately taking a longer way to U Hall— left them with their talk of parties and parties, with their ruby velvets and their silver tulles. I was cold (it had been cold so long!) and I shrank as I went up the scalloped steps to U Hall. I did not want to go up those steps. What was I doing here, anyway, going to a class in Eighteenth-Century Lit? I wasn't especially interested in the eighteenth century. I was interested in my own century, even though I didn't understand it very well, even though you saw one thing in the newspapers and heard another on the street. Why was I going to class? Was this what I was going to do all my life—go to class? I saw myself year after year, trudging back and forth, with no one calling me up but Pinky Carlin. I remembered Charla's warning about Pinky's drinks. It was quite true that I occasionally took one, and everyone knew what *that* meant—one drink led to another! Not only would I be trudging back and forth, my green bouclé sagging by now, and hanging unfashionably beneath my coat, but I would no doubt be weaving drunkenly on my way. The picture made me giggle, yet I was depressed.

I had seldom been so depressed.

The halls were slippery with tracked-in snow, and there were black footsteps everywhere; the paint on the walls, as I went up the stairs, was peeling, and I remembered my father saying that the University could not afford to keep up the buildings as they should. What was the matter with everything, anyway? Why were there black footsteps in the halls, and why was the paint peeling—and why couldn't we wear corsages any more? (For a while I had saved all my corsages: gardenias tied with silver, spicy carnations, baby orchids—I had kept them until they turned yellow and brittle.) There I went, I told myself in horror, thinking about corsages. No social consciousness at all. I was as bad as Charla with her two fur coats. In fact, if I'd been able to get any kind of job, I probably would have bought myself a fur-trimmed costume suit; I was dying for a costume suit.

I went into class and settled myself behind the Eatons, who were a married couple. They were the only married couple I knew and I had always been curious about them.

"Don, I *know* we were right in using the furniture money to start the magazine," Chucky Eaton was saying excitedly to her husband. "It just might get you your fellowship."

"Don't count on it, Chucky," Don answered her.

But she would "count on it," I knew. Chucky Eaton counted on everything.

She said something else to Don in a low voice, and I heard his answering laughter. It seemed to me that they were always laughing. I had been to the Eatons' apartment several times to stay with Bump, their baby. The apartment was bare and plain, but they didn't care.

My friend Jenny rushed in just as class started, a yellow scarf flying from her Harris Tweed coat. She was late because she waited on tables at the dormitory where she lived, but when I turned to grin at her I saw that she was rosily smiling.

I sighed. No one I knew really worried about the headlines in the paper. It was all very puzzling.

At noon I walked across campus with Jenny, who looked as cheerful as always but who did complain about her friend Francis ("That boy worries me because he's always saying he's going to kill himself; of course people who say that never *do*, even when they're in the School of Music"), and then started home. I did not want to go home. I especially did not want to eat lunch at home, but I had no money for the milk shake and olive-nut sandwich I would have preferred at the State Street Drugstore. As I went in my door I could hear my brother arguing with Abby about Roosevelt; and my father, out on the glassed-in sun porch with my mother, was talking—was he?—yes; about *me*.

"All that girl thinks about are clothes, boys, and parties," he said. "It's unbelievable."

"Well, I'm glad she *is* finally interested in clothes." My mother was defending me. "For years she didn't care what she had on—don't you remember what a tomboy she used to be? She was the center on the neighborhood football team."

"Well, that's more than she is now," said my father. "She's just drifting." I could hear him sigh. "She isn't really interested in her graduate work. I'd like to see that girl get a job."

But if I got a job, he would say that I was taking bread out of someone's mouth.

"I wish she'd meet some nice boy," said Mother.

From the kitchen, I could hear Bud intone,

"The New Deal is really *sound*, Abby," while Abby chopped madly away at a salad.

I knew what the salads were like when Bud argued with Abby.

I opened my purse and searched frantically in the cluttered bottom—sometimes I found a coin or so, wadded in a hanky or stuck on a gum wrapper. I did! A quarter and a dime.

I left for State Street.

My father's remarks about my aimlessness, which were quite correct, got me to thinking. I wanted very much to get a job. The trouble was that I could not imagine anyone hiring me.

I felt very inadequate.

I went into the drugstore and settled myself and ordered, thinking *What can I do?* A boy came in and sat down at a nearby table; he looked at me, rather fixedly.

"Do you want the catsup?" I asked.

"No," he said. "I don't want the catsup."

Charla would have said he was staring, but I didn't feel that he was staring. At least, I hoped I didn't think so. I hoped I wasn't getting—peculiar.

How could I get a job? Did I have any assets at all?

I had always gotten "A's" in English, and I had a good, steady "B" average. I was healthy. I had once won every event in a Panhellenic swim meet, including the breast stroke, which I had never swum before. My assets were a "B" average and good health. However, this seemed like rather flimsy equipment.

Moodily, I drank my milk shake and ate my olive-nut sandwich. It was time I got out in the outside world. Friends had written me that the outside world was not the way you thought it was, and they sounded disappointed, and dead tired. But I still wanted to get out myself, be disappointed myself, be dead tired myself, if I had to be.

Before going to the Graduate Reading Room, I stopped in U Hall and looked at the bulletin board near the Placement Bureau. I had looked at it before, but I had never seen anything under the "Job Opportunities" label that seemed at all promising. Usually the jobs were teaching jobs. I was fanatic about not wanting to teach. Both my parents were teachers—my mother had once taught Greek— and Bud planned to teach marine biology. I would do something else.

"Case Workers Wanted," read a sign.

I looked at it, hope prickling my hairline.

I'd had a "minor" in sociology as an under-graduate. "Case Workers." I read the description carefully. "No experience necessary. We will train you. Must have A.B. degree; some background in sociology desirable but not necessary."

I had a background in sociology. In fact I had lived, breathed, and eaten sociology for years. My father had written textbooks on sociology, and I had met sociologists in my home, and we were always getting magazines and books on sociology. Of course, I had paid very little attention to all this surrounding, invading, and buzzing atmosphere. Still . . . I carefully marked down the place where the interviews were to be held. I would go. And if I could get that job, I would take it.

I did not tell anyone at home about my plans.

For one thing, there would be too much comment. (I sometimes envied Jenny, in her tiny cell of a dormitory room, with no one to comment.) Bud, in particular, would be discouraging. Bud had said only the night before that I was like all glamour girls, nothing between the ears. (We'd had a fight.) I would keep entirely silent.

By the time I got home I was so excited about the possibility of getting a job I had to forcibly calm down. "Tranquilize myself," as Jane Austen put it in her novels.

I sat tensely through dinner as my father listened to Abby praise Father Coughlin ("Enough to make a man take to drink," he complained to my mother afterward) and as my brother talked about the changing habits of sea otters. My mother began speculating on the kind of art we might have had during the Middle Ages if it hadn't been for The Church, and my father talked about the spendthrift policies of the twenties (plowing up too much land, investing too much money) and how we were suffering from the effects of this, now.

I didn't say anything. It wore me out just to listen to the rest of them talk.

"Oh, Margie," my brother called, as I left the table. "I have a friend who wants a date with you. He's going to call you."

"I wish you wouldn't call Marjorie *Margie*," my mother said. "Her name is *Marjorie*. —We had a sow on the farm named Margie," Mother explained to Abby, as I cleared the table after dessert.

I was terribly tired of hearing about that sow, and I couldn't imagine my mother on a farm.

"I know you don't like blind dates, Margie. But really, this guy is super," Bud said.

Bud was trying to make up with me because of our fight. It was sweet of him, but I was dubious.

"Bud—" I sighed.

The last time Bud had gotten a date for me, the boy had been shorter than I, his name had been Tristan, and he had taken me on a hike with the Advanced Outing Club. Charla had found out about it, and people were still asking me about the Advanced Outing Club.

"No, Tom's different," Bud insisted. "You'll like him."

Oh, well, what did I have to lose? I wasn't having many dates.

"O.K.," I said. "Fix me up. If he's over three feet tall and doesn't drool, I'll go."

"Marjorie." Mother sighed.

" '. . . three feet tall . . . doesn't drool . . .' " This struck Bud as hilarious; he almost collapsed.

"How's old Charla doing?" he asked finally, recovering himself. "Is she all dated up for the Winter Prom?"

I hesitated, standing there in the hall. She wasn't dated up, but the only reason to tell Bud this was so that he could ask her to Winter Prom, and he wouldn't. He never went to those big parties. Besides, Charla had wrecked her chances with Bud the year before. He had asked her to a football game and dance, and she had accepted, but she'd had a chance to go to the game with a boy who would take her to a tea dance and another party, afterward. She'd

called and said she had this splitting head-
ache. . . .

"Old Charla the Harlot," Bud said cheerfully.

"Bud," my mother said severely. "I won't
have that kind of language around here!"

The phone rang, and I raced upstairs to try
to get it on the extension. The main phone was
in the dining room, under everyone's nose. The
call was for me, but I couldn't think who it was,
at first; I didn't know anyone named "Tom."
Then I remembered: Bud's friend. Bud's
friends were hardly ever named anything like
"Tom." I became hopeful. Tom said he
was doing graduate work in Architecture,
and he wanted me to go to the Beaux Arts
Ball.

"It's a new party we've dreamed up. We're
tired of never having any parties around here.
We're only having a local orchestra—" He hesitated.

"Well, there's nothing wrong with that," I
said hastily. Those girls this morning, I remem-

bered, had been talking about a Beaux Arts
Ball.

"We're wearing artist smocks," he went on,
his voice lightening. "That's so nobody will
know we don't own tails. And you girls can
wear whatever you want. —Costumes, if you
want."

"It sounds like fun," I said.

I liked his voice.

"Your brother really complimented you the
other day, Margie," he said. "Bud tells me
you're a regular glamour girl."

Oh, dear.

"You don't understand," I wailed. "That's
the worst thing Bud can say about anybody."

This, from the sounds he was making, apparently struck him as very funny. There was one
thing about Bud and his friends; they were
easily amused.

He told me when he would be picking me up
the next Friday, and we said good-bye.

I went in to take my bath feeling exhila-
rated.

Margie

We had to schedule baths rather carefully at our house, because although there was a small bathroom downstairs and a shower in the basement, the upstairs bathroom had the only tub. I had complained about this for years, because I liked to pour all sorts of things in the tub and loll there, but there was no time to loll when someone was pounding on the door. Tonight, for instance, my parents were going to some sort of faculty reception, and Bud had said that he was going out. I hurried.

"—perfectly ridiculous that we only have one tub," I complained to my mother, as I emerged in my robe to find her waiting.

"If rushing through a bath is the worst thing that ever happens to you, you're lucky," my mother said tartly. "I still think this house is heaven."

I pondered on her remark as I dressed. I liked our house; it was comfortable and homey, but I didn't see how anyone could call it heaven. It was a brownish, squashed-looking house without much yard, and it had no particular style of architecture. My parents had bought it because it had a small study for my father, was near campus, and had plenty of bedrooms.

I dressed. I got into my black "formal" with the white bateau neckline; it had black crepe roses at the waist and fitted me almost as well as my own skin. Actually, because it was cut on the bias, it was not as tight as it looked; it had hidden pleats and was easy to dance in. Pinky was a very good dancer. Morrie, Charla's date, was nice about dancing with Charla's friends, and was the best dancer I knew. When you were gliding around the floor with Morrie, you were sure that you looked like a John La Gatta illustration in a magaine, very slinky and willowy, if only for that moment, at that time, with that dancer.

My mother knocked on the door to tell me good-bye. She was all ready; she always got ready for parties very quickly, before my father could find some excuse not to go.

"Well, Marjorie, you look very nice."

"Thank you. So do you."

My mother had on her lace, which was what she always wore to a reception.

"But those roses are *wrong*," she said now, frowning at me. She hadn't liked them the day we'd bought the dress. "You don't need all those black roses."

I shook my head. The more roses the better, as far as I was concerned.

My father, now, was looking in.

"Can you sit down in that thing?" he asked.

"*Certainly* I can sit down in it," I said.

It was really very slinky.

They said good-bye and to have a good time, and left, and after I was sure they were out of the house I curled my eyelashes and brushed mascara on them. I had just a few drops of Shalimar perfume left in the bottle—I hadn't gotten any perfume that Christmas, which meant I would have to wait for more until summer and my birthday; I used exactly half of it. I'd save the rest for the Beaux Arts Ball. I was putting on the long rhinestone earrings that matched the buckles on my shoes when Bud looked in.

"You have been getting dressed for two whole hours," he said. "To go out with a dope like Pinky."

"To go to a party," I corrected him. "Bud, don't you ever go to any parties, any more?"

"My year in the cold, cruel world spoiled me for those parties, Margie."

He had left home the year before to bum around the country; he had hitchhiked from coast to coast and even ridden rails.

"I'll bet it was very *interesting* in those hobo jungles," I said. "I'd really like to hear all about it sometime, Bud. It's about time I learned about things."

"You would not like to hear about it, Margie," he said. "And when you do find out about things, you're not going to like them."

He stared at me and shook his head.

"You've got on everything but the kitchen *sink*."

"I suppose you want me to go around looking like Tintern Witherspoon!"

"You couldn't look like Tin Pan if you

tried," he said. "But I don't see why you want to look like a dime-a-dance girl."

I looked around for something to throw at him. The Modern Library Jane Austen—no, I simply could not throw Jane Austen. *War and Peace*—there was a nice fat book. I threw it at him.

He caught it.

"Marjorie *Jones*," he said, horrified. Any book was sacred, to Bud. You did not throw books. "Say, I haven't read *War and Peace* since high school—guess I'll read it again." He looked down at it and then glanced at me. "Boy, I got homesick," he said. "I damned near died, Margie. . . ."

"It must have been awful, Bud."

But there was no way for me to know how it had been.

"Well, guess I'll go to my room and spend the evening with Natasha," he said. "There was a girl with a lot on the ball." He went off, whistling.

I finished getting ready for my date. There

had been no point in explaining to Bud why I was going to so much trouble for someone I cared nothing about; he was a boy. If you were a girl, you wanted to go out. There was the chance that you might meet someone interesting.

Pinky always called for you in a taxi. As he was not registered as a student, the Auto Ban at the University did not apply to him and he could have driven a car, yet he never did. (Perhaps this was to keep up the fiction that he was a student; Pinky did everything possible to give the appearance of a student except, of course, actually go to class.) He was on time, and I was ready, and I chattered amiably as we went to his place. My forte was keeping a conversation going. I was not, really, a campus glamour girl; I was a kind of minor clown. Yet most of the time I had done very well. —Until everyone graduated; until it all changed; until, abruptly, the party was over.

"Those Alps," Pinky said now, in the taxi. "Somebody's Old Man always shells out. . . .

They had Little Jack Little, last time. For a *fraternity* party!"

Anything Pinky went to, or anyone he knew, any tie he wore or drink he mixed, had to be remarkable in some way. And yet Pinky himself was not at all unusual. He was neutral looking. He was washed out, toned down, not quite beige; it was always startling to see Pinky in tails.

We pulled up at the house that contained Pinky's apartment. It was right across from the dorm where Jenny lived, and I wondered if she was working at the "glass machine" in the kitchen, her evening job, with a book propped up in front of her. (I hoped, if she was, she would keep an eye on it; she'd dropped a library book into that machine the week before.)

". . . these babes are all transfers from Vassar," Pinky said now. "I suppose they're here because it's cheaper." He was talking about some girls who would be with us that night. Pinky always had the dope on everybody.

I could see two girls just getting out of a taxi,

one in a fur jacket and velvet, one in a satin evening coat trimmed with ermine. Music was playing from a radio, and the girls were laughing.

". . . no *wonder* I was having trouble with that course. I'd gotten in the wrong *room*," a voice screamed. "It *wasn't* French 31, it was *Sanskrit!*"

I laughed with them. I didn't know them yet, but I waved and laughed as we floated up the steps, with the diamond-packed hardness of snow all around us.

A girl brushed by me as we went into the house and went on up the stairs. She was carrying a bottle of milk and a loaf of bread.

I didn't speak; I couldn't; I was too surprised. The girl was Nan Perry. Nan had been the only really beautiful girl in our high school class. ("*Almost* like Nan—nearly like Nan Perry," people would say; or: "Of course, not as gorgeous as Nan. Not like *that*.") Nan's hair was only brown, as mine was; her eyes were only gray, as mine were—half the girls in America must have gray eyes—but she did not look like anyone else. There was a petal-like shine about her, a glow.

"What's wrong?" Pinky asked me.

"Nothing," I said.

Nan was not in satin or velvet, and no music moved with her. She had an old coat pulled around her, and although she was as lovely as ever, she looked different. I knew that Nan was supposed to be "living" with a boy ("living with a boy"! If that didn't sound exciting!) , but Nan merely looked married, marred, miserable.

"Didn't her old man jump out of a window?" Pinky asked harshly, beside me. "Lost his business or something?"

"Yes," I said, a fishbone, throat-sticking yes. We went into his apartment, where he had all the different bottles waiting beside the little glasses.

Nan's father had been one of the few men in town to be among the suicides right after the crash. Her mother was now in a mental institution, and an older sister was supposedly "raising" Nan. I had not seen her in years. It was Charla who had told me that Nan was "living"

with somebody. Charla had been rather fasci-
nated, and frank enough to say so. She'd never
known anyone who was living with someone.

"What's the matter with you?" Pinky asked.

"Nothing, Pinky. Nothing's the matter."

Others came crowding into the apartment;
names flashed back and forth.

"Oh, *this*," said the girl in satin and ermine.
She had thrown off her coat to reveal a dress of
the same material and cut. It fell to the floor in
a shimmering line. "I had to get it for my party,
so I might as well wear it." She laughed, wrin-
kling up her nose. "What a bore *that* was," she
said.

"She's a debutante," Pinky hissed in my ear.
"So's the one right next to her."

I might have known. Both these girls had
managed a quick tan during a Florida holiday,
and their shoulders were a cream-colored
tawny. They wore what could have been real
pearls, I noticed nervously, and they did not
have cloth roses at their waists. Maybe my roses
were wrong.

"I told you to take tomato juice."

It was Charla, scolding me—I hadn't even seen her come in. There I was with one of Pinky's drinks, which I had apparently taken a sip of. Yes, I had. There was a cough-medicine taste in my mouth.

I really did not want the drink, but I didn't know what to do with it.

"You'd better watch out," Charla told me, under cover of the party talk. "Remember that time you had too many beers, when we were playing baseball at that picnic? We were in a meadow by a brook. —By a *brook*," she repeated significantly.

"I did not have too many beers—"

I was indignant but I did not go on; as there was a pause in the conversation, my voice boomed out with frightening loudness. I remembered what she referred to very well. Although it was true that a great deal of beer had been consumed that day, as a keg of beer had been placed on first base (most of the outs had been made at first), I had not been drunk. Someone had started reciting Housman's lines about rose-lipt maidens and brooks too broad for leaping, and on a sudden impulse I had tried to jump over the brook. It had been wider than I'd thought, and I'd fallen in.

I considered this as I put down the drink.

"Did you see Nan on the stairs?" Charla asked me now, tensely.

"Yes," I said, forgetting about drinks and picnics. "I saw her."

"Oh, *gosh*—" Charla's voice blurred.

For once, I felt in tune with Charla. She had felt what I'd felt.

"Margie, I'd forgotten about Nan. Not her, really—" Charla's face had lost its glaze "—but —I mean—*you* know."

I knew.

You forgot about people like Nan.

"And of course I just adore it here," the girl in velvet was saying. "I mean, you have such a good time. Daddy wants me to graduate from Vassar—you know, go back—but after a Big-Ten school you don't want to go back. It's the parties, I guess."

"You really don't mind leaving those hallowed, ivy-colored walls?" Charla was asking.

Charla had felt what I'd felt for a moment, but she had shaken it off. These girls impressed her.

"Dear old hallowed walls," the satin-ermine one said, lifting her glass. "Dear old ivy."

"It's a good thing to go there first," the girl in velvet said. "If you go to it first, it's all right."

They sounded young to me. Childish, almost. *They* sounded young? But wasn't I young, too? —Not that young. Not any more.

There was another party going on in an adjoining apartment, and we heard singing:

" 'Oh the Dutch family is the best family
That ever came over from old Germany.' "

"Drink . . ." a boy was yelling. "She loves it!"

You were supposed to drain the glass, then, which was quite a feat, considering what might be in it.

"I remember *you* doing that once," said Charla, looking at me.

She was quite right. I had done it, once, to see what it was like. I had gotten sick.

The people in the next apartment did not sound as though any of them would get sick, at least not right away; all you heard was laughter.

I was thinking about toasts and drinking and the one time I had gotten sick after drinking. I was not thinking about Nan Perry, I realized. I was not feeling what had happened to her; even Nan, one of my contemporaries, could not make the headlines come alive.

"You're awfully quiet tonight," Pinky said, rather crossly.

I was not supposed to be quiet. I was supposed to chatter.

The laughter from the next apartment became deafening.

Pinky had been telling everyone that he had bought a darned nice tie on Main Street for only a dollar, and walked into Van Tyles, on State Street, wearing it, just to see their faces, as they had the same tie at two fifty. "But I felt lousy about it. I'll hardly be able to face Van, tomorrow. It wasn't worth it; it made me feel so rotten."

He looked at us expectantly.

It was a boring story, as were most of Pinky's stories. We all smiled, stiffly, while the laughter a wall away bombarded us.

Too many parties had been held in this room. Too many of the same stories had been told, and the windows, I was sure, had never been opened.

There was a single but quite terrifying moment of silence.

"Well," Pinky said briskly, getting up. "On to the brawl."

There was chatter about going on to the Alp House, and did we need a taxi, and that of course we did not, it was right on the corner. Charla and the other girls and I went into the bedroom to get our coats.

"This really isn't for evening wear, but I guess leopard looks pretty good with this red," Charla was saying, slinging on her coat.

It did, although Charla would have looked

almost as good in a burlap sack, a slicker—
anything.

Going down the stairs, I noticed the boys
who were with the debutante-eastern-transfers.
They looked young to me. When had people
started to look young? A sadness clutched at me,
corkscrewing through me, buzzing at my ears, a
sadness that had nothing to do with Conditions
or Headlines or Nan Perry.

Once outside, I shook it off; while we had
been at Pinky's, in that very short time, fresh
snow had fallen. These flakes were different
from the icy stingers that had pecked at me that
morning. They were big, fluffy, musical-comedy
flakes, falling softly with a faint hissing sound.
They touched you and clung to your eyelashes.
They were like flowers. On the sidewalk in
front of the apartment house was a long, narrow
sweep of ice where someone had run and slid
almost to the end of the block, moving the new
snow to one side in a ridge, leaving dark ice free
for the next one who wanted to try it; I couldn't
resist; I broke away from Pinky and ran, jump-
ing on it expertly and turning my feet a little to

one side, balancing myself with my arms. It was a reaction, I suppose, to the stuffy room upstairs, to the stale smoke smell and the cough-medicine drink. Anyway, the slide seemed like a good idea. It wasn't. I hadn't realized that I would go on and on, the snow clearing itself away before my buckled shoes in shining spurts, the black trees rising above me. At first it was so much fun I screamed, but in an instant I could hear the tone of my scream change. I was frightened. I was headed right for an intersection, and I couldn't stop.

"Margie!" I could hear Charla call, exasperatedly.

A tall figure—I could see only the outline of his coat and the slant of his hat—stepped from behind a tree. I saw the bright arc of a cigarette as he flipped it away, and I saw him move in front of me and brace himself. He caught me. I could smell the agreeable smell of a man's coat, a cold, rough, outside smell.

"Where," he asked, "did you think you were going?"

I shook my head, laughing, relieved.

"Thank you," I said.

"Take it easy, Bright Eyes." I couldn't see his face, but I was sure he was smiling. "I might not be around next time." He gave my shoulders a little shake and strode off into the snow.

"I don't know what has gotten into you tonight," Pinky said, coming up behind me. "I told these girls you were one of the most outstanding people on campus—that you were—" He hesitated. Pinky always had trouble making himself understood. "That you were *funny*. Funny ha ha, not funny peculiar. But you were certainly acting peculiar."

"I'm sorry, Pinky," I said. I was not really sorry. That wild slide through the snow, the dark trees, the fear, and then an unknown stranger catching me . . . Who was he? How would I find him again? There were a lot of men around who were tall and who had a certain slant to their hats. You could hardly find anyone by the smell of cold on his coat.

"Margie!" Charla was scolding me. "Here are these girls from an eastern school—*dignified*—and you are acting like an idiot."

"Am I really?"

"They have a different idea of things out in the East, Margie."

I didn't believe that this was true. My friend Chucky Eaton had gone to Wellesley, and Chucky was always hurtling in and out of class or shouting at her husband—Chucky was not especially dignified.

Impervious to Pinky's carping and Charla's scolding, I walked on into the Alp House. I felt light and almost transparent. The stranger would find out who I was and call me; I would meet him some way; we would find each other. I liked his voice (had I heard that voice before?) and I had even liked being called "Bright Eyes," although there was nothing terribly original about it. I felt as though I were floating. Something good was bound to happen.

Music met us as we went into the Alp House. It wasn't Little Jack Little, but it was a good orchestra.

"*Mar*-gie," the orchestra blared out.

"I'm always *think*-ing of you, *Mar*-gie."

Could they be playing that song for me, I wondered? I was still floating. *I* was Margie. What had that tall boy done, catching me under the trees?

"Oh, no!" screamed a girl with swinging blond hair. Stars dropped from her ears. "Just because I'm Margie they always *play* that! Always!" She threw out her arms.

The orchestra had played for that girl, that flashing girl. The music had not been for me. I felt a smile stick on my face like a piece of adhesive. The jewel-like moment in the snow was leaving me fast.

I wished that I had gone on home, called a taxi, kept that moment.

"Come on," said a voice. "Got to leave our coats."

We went down the hall and into a room.

"I almost wish I had gotten a white fur," Charla said, looking critically at her leopard-skin coat as she put it on a chair. "Of course, they gave me some leopard scraps to have made into a toque, which will be darling. But a white fur would be nicer for parties."

"I'm getting sick of parties," I said, without thinking.

"Like fun you're sick of parties," whispered Charla.

She was probably right. I was not really sick of them; I merely thought that I was sick of them. After tonight (the stranger would not call) I would be as anxious as ever to go to parties. I would rush to the phone. I would take two hours to get dressed. I would go out whenever I could. There I would stand, wearing the wrong roses, waiting for music that was not for me.

"How is Bud doing?" asked Charla in a loud voice. "That's Margie's brother," she added quickly to the others. "Smart—oh, *heavens*. How *is* Bud, Margie? He's been neglecting me."

"I don't know how Bud is," I said crossly. "The last time I saw him I threw a copy of *War and Peace* at him."

"Gets 'A's' and never cracks a book," Charla explained over my shoulder.

"Well, I tried to crack him with a book tonight," I said, which I thought was rather a clever little remark, but which went unnoticed as a horde of other satin-ermine girls came in the door.

"Let's *go*," Charla said, in an irritated voice. "The boys are waiting."

The Alp House was one of the biggest of the fraternity houses. They gave their party before the weekend of Winter Prom, just to be different, and they always had a well-known orchestra, and often girls came from out of town for this party.

"The Beaux Arts Ball is not going to be anything to go to at all," Pinky was saying. "Now, this party has tradition, and the Winter Prom has tradition. You need—well, you need *tradition*."

The dance floor was already crowded with couples, and around the edges were the usual number of stags waiting to "cut in." They were looking over the dancers judiciously, rather like shoppers looking around a store before making a purchase. I suddenly found the system annoying. The thought had never occurred to me before.

"Come on," said Pinky.

"Dancing in the dark . . ." wailed the music.

" 'Til the tune ends . . ."

Beside my ear, Pinky began talking with his usual solemnity.

"If you plan it very carefully, you can go to a movie every week night and not repeat," he said.

It was very tiresome talking to Pinky, or even listening to him. Talking to Pinky was like dancing with a poor dancer (one foot gets tireder than the other, and you wonder if the music will ever stop). No matter what Pinky said, I had heard it before.

The music was good. The boys I danced with danced well, and one or two boys I hadn't met before did cut in on me, but all this had also happened before. I could not capture a party feel. Perhaps, instead of pretending to be tired of parties, I was actually becoming tired of them.

"Got a bottle upstairs," said a voice.

I was dancing with a boy who had just described to me, twice, a certain end run of Puzinski's as "the best of his entire career."

"Come on," he said. "If you'd like a little change."

I told him no, the music was much too good.

There was an intermission, and while drinking some unspiked punch (the Alps had gotten into a little trouble at their last party) Charla drew me aside to go to what was designated as "the little girls' room."

"Watch Pinky," she said. "He's had too much. He must have brought a flask with him . . . watch out. I just finished dancing with him, and he about strangled me."

"Oh?" I said.

"Margie, you know what I mean."

She meant that Pinky might try to "make" me. Charla always thought that boys were trying to "make" her, and had had, she'd told me, some very narrow escapes.

"I cannot imagine Pinky being that energetic," I said.

"Just remember that I warned you." Charla

frowned. "In fact, if I were in your shoes, I'd call a taxi and go on home."

I was certainly not going to go home.

Beside us a girl in a very low-cut dress was staring sadly at herself in a mirror.

"Those awful boys stare at you so before they cut in," she wailed. "I'm surprised they don't pinch you or measure you, or something. They *leer.*"

She was quite right. They did leer. I had never noticed it before. I had never had quite as many of them suggest going upstairs before, either.

Pinky was waiting for me in the hall. "C'mere," he said. "Let's have a little something."

Charla had been right. Pinky had brought along a flask, and he had had too much. I tried to feel alarm, but could not. Pinky had always reminded me of a canned pear.

"Let's go in the kitchen a minute," he said.

I did not really want to go home in a taxi. Of course, I didn't want to go in the kitchen, either, but perhaps Pinky simply wanted to talk—he seemed in a talkative mood—and in a few minutes would be back to normal, or, if not, at least as normal as he ever was. I let him lead me away.

"You think you're so smart, with all those guys cutting in on you," he said. "You came with me, and you're supposed to dance with me."

There were several things wrong with this remark. In the first place, I had not gotten nearly the rush from the stags that the other girls had gotten, and in the second, Pinky had an absolute terror of being "stuck" with a girl; if no one else had danced with me he would have been desolate. He was clearly not himself.

We were now in the enormous kitchen of the Alp House, which was lit by a single bulb hanging over the dark expanse of stove. Huge saucepans and great, moon-shaped skillets hung on the wall. The place made me think of a deserted castle in a fairy tale; at any moment we would hear a giant's footsteps clumping toward us.

Pinky had pushed a glass toward me.

"First we'll have a little drink," he said, "and then we'll go back to my place."

"No," I said. "We will not."

"Now *Margie*." His voice had lightened with the friendly tease of camaraderie. "Now Margie."

He leaned forward. Pinky, I was abruptly aware, was getting out of hand. I moved a few steps away.

"There's your drink," he said.

"I'm afraid you'll have to down both of them, Pinky." It was an effort to keep my voice light and gay.

"Margie—"

I could smell the rotten apple smell of liquor on his breath, and the egg-white pale face was coming closer. The kitchen was empty. I should feel alarm, I realized; a lot of alarm. It had been stupid to come in here with Pinky. In fact, it had been stupid to go out with Pinky. I had better leave. As Pinky drank both his drink and mine, it occurred to me that this was a lot of whisky. I turned and ran.

Charla and Morrie were out in the hall.

"Where have you been?" asked Charla.

"Sweet little *Margie*," said a voice behind me. "Nobody gets to first base with Margie."

I turned; it was Pinky.

"You do not," he said severely, "know what the score is."

I backed off. I could feel people staring, and heard the chalk-going-the-wrong-way sound of a girl's giggle.

"You little—"

Pinky called me a name that was unfamiliar to me, although I had a fair idea of what it meant. Then he fell, grabbing for me. One hand clutched my dress. The material gave way with a sickening, almost slushy sound; black crepe petals swirled about me and fell at my feet.

"*Margie*." It was Morrie, running toward me and looking at Pinky as he went by. "Go get her coat for her, Charla—"

"Could you take me home, Morrie? Or call a taxi—"

My voice sounded all right.

I stood there, looking down at the floating black petals.

Morrie took me home. I was glad it was Morrie, because he was one of the nicest boys I knew, and would make no remarks about the incident.

"Something like this happens to everybody at least once," was all he said. "Don't worry about it."

"I won't."

"He just had too much, Margie. Don't let it bother you. —I don't think he meant to tear your dress . . . that's too bad, about your dress."

"It doesn't matter," I said.

I thanked him as he walked me up to my door. I even made some silly remark about the fact that Charla would miss him.

"Yes, the poor kid'll be brokenhearted." He grinned.

Inside, everything was quiet. Bud had apparently deserted Natasha and gone out after all; I didn't hear his radio going. I went on upstairs.

It wasn't until I was standing in my room that I began to shrivel. And then it was not because of the name Pinky had called me; it was not any one thing; it was a combination of things . . . the appraising glances of the stag line, and the voices suggesting that we go upstairs, and the weariness of making chatter to dopes like Pinky Carlin.

There was a car in the driveway. My parents were coming home; I could hear the final wheeze of the Hudson before it lurched into the garage.

Still, I stood there.

"Margie?" My mother called, when they came in. "You're home?"

"Yes," I said.

"Did you have a good time?"

"Oh, *yes*," I said. "I had a wonderful time."

You always said that you had a wonderful time.

I took off the ruined dress and stared at it. There would be no way to fix it or repair it. I didn't think I would want to wear it again, anyway.

I would not, I decided, go to any parties for a while. I would take myself out of circulation and just sit tight. There were other things in life besides parties; there must be.

As I dropped off to sleep that night, I remembered my slide on the ice and the tall boy who had caught me. It was dreamlike and unreal now, just as those falling flakes had been unreal. Had it really happened? Had someone stepped out of the dark and caught me, or had I made it all up?

The next Monday I set off through the blowing cold, gloomily conscious of the fact that I was poorly prepared for an examination and that weekends, from now on, were going to be dull. I stopped at a bookstore near the campus to buy the "blue book" that would record my sketchy knowledge of Defoe and Smollett. Reaching into my purse for a nickel, I found only the usual litter. I was out of money, and I had forgotten to get any from my parents or from Bud.

The owner of the bookstore was a family

friend but I didn't see him anywhere. A squirrel coat brushed by me. "Tintern!" I called.

Tintern Witherspoon's lean face turned toward me unsmilingly.

"Brother, can you spare a nickel?" I asked. "Not a dime, just a nickel?"

"I'm late *now*," she said harshly, and left.

Someone ran into me. I turned around to see Chucky Eaton's shaggy raccoon coat.

"Need a blue book, Margie?" she asked. "Here! I have an extra one."

She gave it to me.

"Oh, thank you, Chucky . . ."

She had already gone.

A person like Chucky always seemed to turn up at the right time. I had been rescued. I had been rescued just as surely as I had been rescued as I slid down the street that snowy night. It was a lucky omen. I felt like exploding; something wonderful might still happen to me. No, I was romanticizing, I told myself sternly. There was no reason to feel that anything wonderful might happen. I must be sensible; I must be a Miss Dashwood.

Margie

I went out into the snow, humming a little. I would never really be a Miss Dashwood. I was going to stay out of circulation for a while, but I was—Margie.

I went on to my exam, which was not as hard as I had feared.

After the blue book, Jenny and I started off down State Street toward her dorm. She had invited me to lunch, as once a week she had a "day off" and could even ask a guest for meals. We were passing the School of Music when she suddenly stopped and grabbed my hand.

"Listen."

I listened.

Someone was playing a concerto, far up there behind the cramped smudge of those faded brick walls, but there was nothing faded or cramped or smudged in this music.

"That's Francis."

"How can you tell?"

"Because no one else around here can play like that."

I listened. She was right.

Bemused, we went to lunch. The stew, the

salad, the paperweight-firm pudding were before us. We settled down to lunch happily; we had passed our exam, and we had heard Francis playing.

Jenny was unlike the students I had met as an undergraduate. She had always had to work to stay in college, and had generally lived in a rooming house or in the corner of someone else's apartment.

"I must say this isn't bad," she said, digging into her stew.

"Where did you eat last year?" I asked her.

"Let's not discuss it." She sighed. "Dinner was a can of tomato soup, heated in a percolator."

I stared at her.

"That's how a lot of students eat—if you can call it eating. Didn't you know?"

I had not known.

"What about Francis?"

"He eats all right." She shook her head and smiled. "—When he remembers to eat."

I left for home after lunch. I had another final the next day, and needed to study for it. As

I started to walk across campus, I waved to a dark-haired, rawboned-looking boy who was just leaving the School of Music. It was Francis, and he returned my wave.

I stared after him as he disappeared into a crowd, and remembered a line from one of Bud's letters which he had written to my father when he was so homesick:

"I can appreciate the University now that I'm away from it . . . mostly because of people like you, Dad . . . people who care, and do, and will go on caring and doing no matter what happens. Not that there are too many like *you*, Dad. . . . Most of us just sit around, at a University, warming our hands at the fire . . ."

Francis was not just keeping warm by a fire. He was one of the ones who stoked the throbbing pulse of this place.

No thought of this nature had ever occurred to me before.

It was rather startling.

The Hudson was in the garage when I got to the house, which meant that my father was there. I went on inside. I knew that he was in his little study, working on his Revision, or in other words redoing his book on Institutions, although nobody felt that this book needed redoing. He was the one who felt it needed redoing.

I tiptoed past his study, although there was no need for me to have tiptoed. He was lost, sitting there at his desk in a shamble of books and papers and clippings; he did not hear me.

The phone rang. I jumped; I was apparently somewhat lost myself.

It was Charla.

"Where have you been?" she demanded.

She had apparently been trying to get me.

"I was having lunch with Jenny," I said. "A friend of mine who works at Angel Quad."

"Well. —Have you recovered from the Alp House thing?"

The Alp House. Pinky.

"Certainly."

"I *warned* you about Pinky."

That was right, she had.

"You should have gone home earlier, Margie. Everyone knows you're All Right, but there have been plenty of girls who were All Right who ended up, somehow or other, with bad reputations."

"I know," I said.

"Now listen." Charla's voice rose. "What is this about your going to the Beaux Arts Ball—a new party bound to be a flop—with a boy you haven't even met?"

I stared at the phone, horrified. I could feel even my nostrils droop; I had completely forgotten about Tom and the Beaux Arts Ball. Just because a party had been mentioned, just because Tom had called, I had committed myself to an evening that would probably be worse than the Alp House evening.

"You'd better break that date," said Charla.

"Well, Bud knows this Tom," I said defensively. It was a habit with me to resist Charla. But even as I spoke, I was remembering Tristan and the Advanced Outing Club.

"Break the date," Charla said again.

"How did you know I was going to the Beaux Arts Ball?" I asked her, realizing that I hadn't mentioned it to her.

"I met this Tom, yesterday. He came over here to ask Daddy's advice about a course for next semester. He told me he was taking you to the Ball."

"Oh?" I was normally curious, in spite of my decision to remain out of circulation for a while. "What's he like?"

"At first glance *fine*," said Charla. "He's tall enough, I must say, and so on. But—" I heard her sigh. "No," she said finally, regretfully. "It's a little hard to explain, but—*no*."

Tom was not All Right.

I told her good-bye and hung up, unhappily aware that Charla, although irritating, was probably giving me good advice. There had been times when I should have taken her advice. But shouldn't I go to just one more party? In the first place, I didn't like to break dates. My normal instinct was to take a chance— follow my impulse, go out with Tom. But where, I thought with misgivings, had my normal and impulsive instincts gotten me? They had dumped me in a brook, once. They had made me down a glass and get sick. They had whisked me down the ice. Of course, someone had caught me there on that ice. . . . "Take it easy," the tall stranger had said. "I might not be around, next time." And probably he wouldn't be around, next time.

I had better take it easy.

I would not go to the Beaux Arts Ball.

Bud came in during the middle of the afternoon, and I met him in the hall and asked him to tell Tom that I could not go out with him that Friday night.

"Listen here, Margie, you do your own dirty work. I suppose somebody's asked you to the Winter Prom! I'll give you Tom's number, and *you* call him."

"Oh, Bud, please," I groaned. "Please. I'd feel so silly! You know him and I don't. Say I'm sick or something. Say anything, but get me out of it. And it's not because I'm going to the Winter Prom. I'm never going to any party again, ever."

"I'm going to take you straight to the Health Service," he said, alarmed. "I *thought* you looked as though you had a temperature."

I burst into tears. There was no rational explanation for my tears, except that I was beginning to find out about things, and, as Bud had predicted, I didn't like it. And he could joke about it. . . .

"Oh, all right, all *right,*" Bud said. "I'll call him. I hate to, though. He doesn't know many people around here. And, Margie, no matter what I say, he'll think you're breaking this date because you have a better one. He'll think you're going to the Winter Prom."

"I wouldn't do a thing like that!"

"No, but there are plenty of girls who would. They take any date as a sort of insurance, then break it if something better comes along."

He knew. It had been done to him.

"Tell him—"

"Look, I'll just tell him. I guess I'll have to . . ." He paused. "What's wrong, anyway?"

"Never mind."

"Did some guy make a pass at you? You know, the way you babes get yourselves up . . ."

"I said never *mind.*"

76

"Now, don't start bawling again, Margie. I said I'd tell him. But it's really too bad. . . . I think you'd like him."

It was too bad.

Bud went downstairs to use the phone, and came back presently, and said, "Done."

"Thank you," I muttered. I sat there and glared at my Chaucer text. I would not be going to the Beaux Arts Ball.

The week of finals was always a sad week, coming as it did in the dead center of winter, after the celebration of Christmas and long before any hint of spring. This exam week was worse than ever before. Winter came too early, I thought; lasted too long; winter started in November, when the cold rain washed even the red out of the maples, and then the snow started. Surely this winter was colder than ever before. The people you passed seemed huddled into themselves; girls swaddled in furs, nuns draped with black; I passed a girl from India wearing a sealskin coat over her sari, and her face was purple. You passed the same people every day. All hours were the same; everything was the same.

It was winter, dead center, solstice. Why couldn't I catch fire? "She's drifting," my father had said, and he was right. I was going to try to get a job, but I did not, even, know much about the job. I wanted the job to try to get me off dead center. I needed a change, a fresh start. I wanted that job for all the wrong reasons.

And yet, paradoxically, the idea of the coming interview warmed and sustained me. It was a secret from my family, for one thing. It was *mine*. Luckily, too, the interview was arranged conveniently for me, right after my last exam. I could go on and register for the next semester and finish my Master's, if I didn't get the job. I was not going to drift any longer; I was going to do *something*.

My Chaucer exam was my last one. I walked into the classroom less chilled than usual because my father had insisted on driving me to campus that day, but I was still numb with gloom. *Chaucer*. What was Chaucer doing in this cold place? The pilgrims had set out for

Canterbury in April, with flowers shooting around them and a holiday feel in the air, hoofbeats clattering, cloaks blowing.

Everyone in the room looked gloomier than I felt. Chucky Eaton sat beside her husband with a drowned, blank face. Jenny, sliding in early for once, had been crying.

"What's the matter?" I asked Jenny.

"Oh—" She stretched out a smashed chocolate heart.

"They have valentines in the dime store, and I thought I'd cheer Francis up (he's worried about his grade in Theory—he had an argument with his professor); and anyway, they have this girl at a counter who decorates chocolate hearts—you know, writes a person's name on it with icing. So I had her write 'Francis' on this for him. But *look*. I must have held it too hard, it's crushed—"

The icing had smudged. Instead of Francis it said 'Fricas.'

"That's the story of my whole life," she groaned. "A Fricas. I can't do anything right!" She stared at the heart in her hand. "And I've gotten chocolate all over my coat, and that coat was *just cleaned.*"

She didn't care about the coat, I knew, but she did care about Francis.

"The chocolate will blend right into the tweed," I said. "And Jenny, Francis won't do anything silly. He's much too intelligent."

I didn't know Francis very well, but I thought I should reassure her.

She sat down, still looking at the smashed heart.

"I'm so afraid that someday he won't call me at four," she said. "He calls every afternoon, you know; we check on each other. We have each other's schedules."

"He'll call," I insisted.

We divided up the heart and ate it, as it was spoiled as a valentine.

The chocolate, or my reassurance, apparently cheered Jenny. She settled down to pore over her notes, but I noticed that Chucky still seemed woebegone.

"See you later," her husband said gruffly, and left to sit in the back of the room.

Chucky continued to sit and stare.

"Chucky—is Bump all right?"

The only time Chucky looked worried was when Bump was sick.

"He's fine." Chucky sighed. "We just left him with the boys downstairs. It's just—oh, Margie, it's so *silly* of me. But we have Patron Tickets to the Winter Prom tonight and it's Hal Kemp—Hal Kemp played for the tea dance the day I met Don . . . but we can't go. We don't have anyone to stay with Bump."

"Can't you leave him with the boys downstairs?"

"No. They're angels to keep him in the daytime. They have an experiment at the lab to check at eleven, and again at two."

"Chucky," I said, "I'll stay with Bump."

"You're going to the Beaux Arts Ball!"

"No, I'm not. I'm not going anywhere."

"Margie, I can't ask you to—"

I knew what she meant; she couldn't pay me.

"Chucky, let me do it. It will make me feel noble and good, and I need to feel noble or good or something."

"You are noble and good!" shouted Chucky.

"Ho *ho,*" said Jenny, beside me. She sounded completely back to normal.

It was a strange experience to spend the night of the Winter Prom in the Eatons' apartment.

I wandered aimlessly around. For some reason, I was unable to sit down and read, although the Eatons' apartment was full of books, and the galleys of their magazine *Contemporary* littered the place. I couldn't concentrate. It was the night of the Winter Prom. It was like the day of a big game; you do not have to go to the game, and you may not even want to go, but if you don't go, there is nothing else that you will be able to do, either.

It was very quiet. I could hear clocks ticking. Even Bump was inconsiderate, and refused to fuss or need changing. I would have welcomed his company.

The Eatons came in about one, which was early for a Prom night, but they were glowing and had "adored every minute of it." Chucky fixed bacon and pancakes, still in her beaded crepe, and we even woke Bump up and gave him some. Then Don walked me home along the white streets. Couples passed us in furs and top hats; a drunk was doing a solitary tap dance under a street light, and laughing girls spilled from taxis.

I woke up the next morning quite cheerful. At least, I told myself serenely, I probably felt better than a lot of other people who were waking up that morning. I dressed and went down to breakfast. I sensed, rather than heard, an odd silence. Was everyone still asleep? No, my father and Bud were sitting at the breakfast table, and I could hear my mother and Abby murmuring, in the kitchen.

"Hide the *Daily*—that's the thing to do," Abby hissed.

Something had happened.

Jenny was so worried over Francis; had he done away with himself! Or had he hurt her! He *couldn't* have! I rushed into the kitchen and grabbed the paper.

"Marjorie," my mother said.

There was nothing on the front page except a

write-up of the Winter Prom and of the various other parties. The *Daily* put out a "Prom Edition" this particular weekend. Puzzled, I put it down. Then a name jumped out at me. *Charla.*

"Charla Meadows was with Tom Kent (Arch. Grad) at the gala new Beaux Arts Ball. . . . Charla was stunning as usual in an Amazon costume trimmed with leopard skin . . . those two were certainly having a good time! This new party promises to become one of the gayest affairs of the post-exam party weekend. . . ."

There is some mistake, I thought. Charla wouldn't have gone out with Tom. And she wouldn't have taken a date at the last minute, like that. She certainly wouldn't have told me not to go out with Tom, and then have gone out with him herself. Charla wouldn't do a thing like that.

"Old Charla the Harlot," Bud said cheerfully.

There was no mistake.

Charla had indeed told me not to go out with Tom, and then gone out with him herself.

"I bet you're mad at her," Abby breathed.

"I'm mad at myself," I said. I was.

I tried to eat breakfast (glad I could explain that it was my second one within twenty-four hours), and, for once, was relieved that my family was talkative. I didn't want to be noticed.

After breakfast I went out into the snow and down the block to Charla's.

Charla lived in a large white house set back behind blue spruces (Mrs. Meadows was said to have Money). The house itself was large and plain, and I always gasped when the maid let me into its suffocating and cluttered interior. There were things jammed on the walls, arrayed on tables, and set under glass.

"Marjorie!" Mrs. Meadows rushed forward. "I do hope Charla is awake. Ah, she had quite a night last night! I don't think that child got in until two, at least. And what a flurry around here getting that costume—Marjorie, you would have died if you'd seen me fussing around here; it didn't come until six o'clock. I was *wild*. And after that, we had to sew the leopard-skin touches on it. It arrived by special delivery—you see, her cousin in Shaker Heights, Mildred Marley, had been in a costume ball last month as an Amazon. Those are the Marleys of Ohio, you know—the Marley Mills—*not* the Grosse Pointe Marleys, although they are related by marriage (not to us, unfortunately). Anyhow, when I saw that the costume was orange, I nearly died; it's the one color Charla couldn't wear even as a child, but she convinced me that with the proper make-up—"

"Mrs. Meadows," I interrupted her, "I'll just run upstairs, and if Charla is asleep I won't disturb her."

Mrs. Meadows looked at me in astonishment. She would probably tell my mother, the next time she saw her, that Marjorie "had interrupted her rather rudely." Mrs. Meadows often complained that she couldn't understand young people nowadays; they never let you finish a sentence.

"All right, dear. You and Charla have always been *such* good friends. Look out, that rug on the landing does slip a little; Charlotte's father is always fussing at me about it, but I tell him that I just don't care; I like things covered up and cozy. I—"

Mercifully, the telephone rang, and the maid called her.

I went on up and tapped on Charla's door, and she said sleepily, "Come in."

Charla's room was done entirely in a sort of Easter-egg pink, and everything had bows on it.

"Why did you do it?" I asked. "Why did you tell me not to go out with Tom Kent?"

Charla sat up in bed, looked straight at me, and gave one small, completely unembarrassed giggle.

"Because I wanted to go out with him myself," she said. "I wanted to go to the Beaux Arts Ball."

I nodded. I'd found out what I'd come to find out.

I turned and left.

"Margie—" she called.

We had known each other a long time. We had played jacks on damp sidewalks under

green leaves; we had gone to dancing school together; we had walked up steps, carefully, on
the way to rush parties.

"Margie—"

I went downstairs.

Mrs. Meadows was still on the phone, and I
escaped out the door, away from the clutter and
chatter. Had I been in a more charitable mood,
I might have reflected that there was plenty of
reason for Charla to be her forthright and pred-
atory self. I was not in a charitable mood.

I had been a dupe, and my anger at myself
was complete. Charla's defection was no real
loss and, once I thought about the situation, not
even surprising; what I minded was that I had
been so foolish. My reasons for accepting Tom's
invitation to the ball had been partly because I
had heard other girls say they were going to it
(shallow, childish) and because I could not resist a party. My reasons for not going were even
worse. Thrown off balance by the dreary evening at the Alp House, I had let myself be influenced by Charla to break a date. Charla wasn't
to be trusted, and I had known that. Why

hadn't I followed my natural impulse? The one time I had been cautious and careful had been the time I should have gone my own way. I had been a fool, and, worse than that, an unkind fool, a mindless fool.

I hurried home and up to my room. It was all so horrible that it was probably funny, although I did not think that I could laugh about it. —Not for a long time, anyway.

"Hey." Bud was outside my door. "I hear the Beaux Arts Ball was quite a superior rat race."

The last person I wanted to see was Bud.

"Too bad you didn't go, dearie," he said. "Too bad you didn't trust your brother's advice."

"I told you I was through with parties," I said with dignity. "There must be something else in life besides *parties*."

"Hey!" he said, concern softening his tone. "Are you all right?"

"Certainly I'm all right. Don't you have to go to Kroger's or count sea horses or something?"

"I just don't understand—"

"I have *stopped* being shallow and frivolous," I almost shouted at him. "You and Daddy are always telling me I'm so frivolous, with nothing on my mind but parties and clothes—I'm going to—be serious," I said.

"You're going to try and be *what?*" asked Bud.

"I'm normal." I was shouting louder now. "I do think of something besides parties. At least, I'm going to *try* to." I sounded, I was sure, like a dope, and I knew that he was coming in to see what was the matter; I hadn't put him off with all my talk.

"Look here," he said, coming in and closing the door. "Nothing's wrong with you, Margie. As I think about it, you are almost abnormally normal. You're all right. —Now, don't start bawling."

I looked at him in surprise. He had said that I was normal.

"Of course you've wanted to go to parties," he said. "You want to meet a man and get your hooks into him—not an easy feat right now, when most males are too worried about getting out and getting started to be hookable. In fact, now that I think about it, it must be rather hard, being a girl."

I swallowed. "It is," I said. His sympathy put me off so that I did not even mind his remark about getting my hooks into a man. Still . . . "But *Bud,*" I said, in a troubled tone. Was he right? Had I just been trying to do what was normal? You never admitted that you were after a man. People would have said you were boy crazy or "fast." What you did say was that you just loved parties and that you always had a perfectly wonderful time, and of course you could say that you hoped to meet someone "interesting." You poured yourself into a shining dress; you dropped stars from your ears; you shook out your few remaining drops of perfume . . . you did all this for just one reason. I could feel a slow blush start up my neck.

"Margie, it's nothing to be ashamed of," Bud said earnestly. "Of *course* you want to go to parties. I think we've been wrong to criticize you. You've simply been going about your business."

I gasped. I knew I was as red as fire.

"There's plenty of precedent for it," Bud said seriously. "Think of the Bennet girls, sitting there with their embroidery frames and talking about their next ball. They could talk about balls; they could discuss Bingley, who had moved into the neighborhood and just might give a party. —But that was all they could do."

"They hoped to meet someone interesting," I said.

"Certainly. —And take Kitty, in *Anna Karenina*, or for that matter Natasha, in *War and Peace*—Natasha didn't have war on her mind, or peace either. Natasha had something entirely different on her mind."

He was right. He was perfectly right.

"Even Cinderella, wanting to go to the ball—why did she want to go to the blamed ball? She wanted to meet the Prince, that was why."

I wondered if Bud meant what he was saying. I looked at him. He did.

"Parties are important for women," he went

on. "After all, they can't publicly go after a guy with a butterfly net or a spear or what have you. They have to go to parties and 'have a good time,' and hope for the best."

He was right. The thought was unique and vibrant enough to cheer me. You went to parties to get a man. For more parties you forsook hallowed, ivy-covered walls; to get to a party you would put up with a bore; to go to a new and possibly good party, you were willing to lie and to cheat and to steal.

I knew now why I had gone out with Pinky. I knew why the girls from the East were here. I even knew why Charla was Charla.

"Wash your face and let's whip," he said.

"Whip? Whip where?"

"There's a Garbo movie at the Majestic, and I'll treat you to a milk shake on State Street."

It rained all next week. This was strange for February, which was usually too cold for rain, but day after day the skies melted, turning the snow to slush, washing all the ice away but a pocked rind. Dampness slid down your neck. Black water from passing cars splashed your stockings.

Tom did not call me. Of course, I hadn't expected he would.

The interview for the case-work job was at the end of the week. Everything was set for my interview in the Placement Office, but to my horror, as I started out, I discovered that my father planned to walk to the campus with me. I didn't want him to find out that I was going to the Placement Bureau because he would be sure to want to know why, and to worm the whole thing out of me, and "help," and then if I did get the job I would always feel that it was his doing. How could I get away from him?

"I just thought it was a nice day for a walk," he said cheerfully, as we splashed along with our one umbrella.

He had left the Hudson on campus after his last class the day before. I knew enough not to mention this, as he was very sensitive about doing anything absent-minded, because he often said that the "absent-minded professor" was just one of those campus myths.

"I understand that you and Charla are not the best of buddies any more," he said.

"No, we are *not* the best of buddies. But then, we never were."

"I thought her choice of an Amazon costume for that party most appropriate," he went on. "Of course, she could have gone as Lucrezia Borgia; that would have been even better."

I giggled as the tipped umbrella let some water down my neck. "Yes, she turned out to be a most loyal friend," I said. "Daddy"—despite the fact that I could partly understand Charla's action, her deception was still a blow—"did you find, at my age, that some things do not seem to make sense?"

"I certainly did," he said. "In fact I find that at *my* age some things do not make sense."

"But some things do," I said hopefully.

"Oh, yes," he assured me. "Some things do. Now let me think. Give me time; I'll think of *something*."

I giggled as he helped me over a puddle.

"Nothing like a good brisk walk in the morning, Marjorie."

"Oh, yes, *delightful*, Daddy."

We were now walking across the campus. Someone had stopped respectfully and said, "Professor Jones?"

It was one of my father's former students, here for some sort of meeting and anxious to ask him about something.

"Yes, yes, that's all very interesting," my father said, after he had introduced me and listened to the man. "The question of whether or not we, a so-called civilized people, can learn from a primitive tribal group. —Now I hope you don't mean in the old romantic sense. After all, poor Rousseau—"

Oh, no, he did not mean in the old romantic sense. Poor Rousseau—

This sounded as though it might go on for some time. I moved away, experimentally. My father was deep in conversation, and rain dripped from his hat.

"Daddy," I said. "I have an appointment."

". . . you take the 'taboo,' for example," my father was saying.

"Daddy." I spoke louder. "It's raining!"

He didn't hear me.

I walked quietly off; he wouldn't miss the umbrella, and in fact he would not even miss me. I felt a little guilty as I went into U Hall with the umbrella, and I looked back; he was still deep in conversation. There was actually no particular reason for me to feel guilty, as he was talking to an attentive listener about a subject they both found fascinating. This was what he meant by some things, at least, making sense.

The Placement Bureau was full. People, apparently, were beginning to get jobs; things were a little better, as my father had said they would be. There were several girls my own age waiting to be interviewed. Among them were Nan Perry and also, to my amazement, Charla.

I sat next to Nan.

"Hello, Nan," I said.

She smiled. "Why, hello, Margie. It's been a while."

It had been a while. I had barely seen her

since high school except for that glimpse before Pinky's party—I had seen her just once, I remembered, now.

I had seen her at a football game. The boy I was with had stopped at a stand to buy me a chrysanthemum, and the girl selling them had been Nan. Our eyes had met; for a scalding second, we had stared at each other; then we had both gasped out "Hi."

I didn't like to think of that encounter. I was sure that she didn't like to think of it, either.

"How's your mother, Margie? And your dad?"

"Just fine."

"Did you ever know that they came over to see me, *twice,* when—when things happened—and offered to take me in?—let me live at your house?"

"No, I didn't know that, Nan."

I wasn't surprised. They had taken in others.

"Are you going after this case-work job, Nan?" I asked. If she was, I was not going to apply. I was not going to take bread out of her mouth.

"No. I understand Charla Meadows, over there, is, but I'm not. I'm after bigger fish than *that*. Fifty bucks a month to train, and then only a hundred and twenty to start? Not me."

For the first time I heard an edge in her voice, a grating roughness. But why shouldn't there be an edge in her voice?

"Look, Margie," she said now, quickly. "We were always good friends—I want you to come to a meeting with me and learn about something, something really *important*. I wouldn't ask just anybody. I don't *trust* everybody. I— here." She handed me a card.

I don't know why I was so surprised.

"I can't, Nan," I said finally. "My father has told both Bud and myself to—well, not to."

He had told us just that. "Young Communist League, Old Communist League, any Communist anything," he had said. "Stay away from it!"

"I suppose your father thinks Roosevelt is going to get the country out of this mess," she said coldly.

"He hopes so."

"Ha! Roosevelt! So he's got a few men digging ditches, a few boys getting a measly dollar
a day at a C.C.C. camp! And that fixes everything! He's swung people away from *us,* that's
all he's done.—*Roosevelt!*"

I had often heard Roosevelt's name spoken in
hatred, but not with such venom.

Nan snapped a book open and turned her
shoulder perceptibly away from me.

I couldn't believe that she was seriously interested in communism. You heard a lot about
students being communists, especially in the
Detroit Free Press and in the *Saturday Evening
Post,* but I had never met a student interested
in communism, and I could not believe that
Nan was interested in it.

Her averted shoulder distressed me more than
her political views.

"But Nan," I began. I couldn't leave things
this way. I was going to ask her for lunch or
dinner, say something, do something; I didn't
want to cut her off.

She looked at me sideways and then went

back to her book. "I'm quite busy," she said. "Nice to have talked to you."

Her shoulder turned further away.

That was that.

I was conscious now of my feet, sopping wet, the clammy feel of my clothes, and of my hair, straggling underneath my collar. The room felt airless and hot. Discouragement weighed me. Here I sat beside a girl who did not want to talk to me, near a girl I did not want to talk to, waiting for a chance at a job I wanted for all the wrong reasons.

Charla was called in for her interview. She was not wearing either of her fur coats; very sensibly, she had on a trim-looking trench coat, and she had toned down her make-up. She was the picture of an earnest young girl going after a really significant job and being really serious. I was in my muskrat, as it was the only warm coat I had, and I was sure that I was wearing too much lipstick. I blotted my lips nervously with a tissue, and waited. I tried to remember what my father had said about social work, to think of some significant phrase that would impress the man I was to see, but my mind was a blank. *I* was a blank, I thought gloomily. A complete blank.

I could hear Charla talking very soberly, very persuasively—the words were muted, but the tone was convincing. Charla would get the job and I wouldn't. Charla had always had more dates than I; Charla never fell in brooks; and Charla had snaked Tom Kent from right under my nose.

"Miss Jones," called a voice.

It was my turn. I got up, creaking.

I went into the little cubicle to face a man who looked very much like my father. (I hoped Daddy was not still standing in the rain, talking about taboos.)

"Sit down, Miss Jones," he said. He was holding my transcript and my Health Service Record. "I like what I see here. You're healthy, and you have a 'B' average."

I sagged with relief. I was, at least, healthy. I got "B's."

"It would be an even better average except

that my father made me take Economics," I said. "And my brother made me take Organic Evolution and Genetics." I had gotten my only "D's" in those courses.

"You must come from an interesting family," he said.

I told him I wasn't sure he was using quite the right word.

He laughed, and I thought dazedly, *He likes me*. Did I have the job?

It wasn't that simple. He asked me what I would do in a number of situations; to one and all I replied, "I don't know." I had to say I didn't know. The problems he posed seemed insoluble.

Then he asked me a question that floored me.

"Times are hard and you would expect the clothing of students to reflect this," he said. "But I notice that the students here seldom go around in dungarees or patched jackets—why?"

He was staring at me intently. He expected me to say something sensible, and something that had required some thought. I was terrified.

"Why don't they look like slobs?" he asked.

I remembered, suddenly, Abby's neat outfits, and Chucky Eaton's beaded dress, and Jenny's coat. There was something terribly sad about Jenny's coat.

"Some of them do not dare look poor," I said finally. "Because they are."

He nodded.

That was all, except that he asked me why I wanted the job, and I told him that I was tired of Graduate Reading Rooms and that I hoped to get out into the mainstream of life a little more. It had occurred to me that perhaps my reasons for wanting this job were not so bad, after all.

He nodded again and handed me a piece of paper.

"When do I start?" My voice was a sort of squeak.

"You won't really 'start' for quite a while, Miss Jones. You will follow, watch, question, and, we hope, learn. Then you'll start. It's all written down right here. By the way, you'd better get yourself some low-heeled shoes. You'll be doing a lot of walking."

"All right," I said, and went out in a daze.

Charla was waiting for me in the hall.

"Did they ask you back?" she snapped, without even saying "hello." "Did they say anything to *you?*"

"I . . ." So I had beaten out Charla, this once.

She snatched the paper out of my hand, read it, and thrust it back.

"Aren't you something, though," she said. "Of course, he probably knew who you were. You're the daughter of the great Professor *Jones.*" She wheeled and strode off.

I watched her go around the corner, and then the perfect comeback burst out (late, as all perfect comebacks are). "Sure," I snapped. "Jones is such an unusual name."

Oh, well.

I had gotten the job. I was going out into the world, for good or bad; my parents would not have to worry about my drifting, and Bud would not have to give me money, and who knew?—I might even turn out to be useful. I rushed home to tell everyone the news.

"You got *what?*" said my mother, who was fitting a slip cover on a chair in the living room. "Marjorie, dear, there must be some mistake."

"What did you say?" Bud was coming down from his room. "Who's going to pay you to do *what?*"

"Forevermore," my mother gasped, looking at the paper. "It says right here she'll be paid fifty dollars and twenty cents a month while in training, and after that a hundred and twenty."

"Let me see that paper," said Bud. I heard him gasp. "Why they *are* going to pay her!"

"Now, you stop that," said my mother. "Poor Marjorie—nobody ever thinks she can do anything, and the way you and your father carry on sometimes, I'm surprised she hasn't gone all to pieces. Marjorie, this is wonderful!"

"Good for you, Margie," said Bud.

My mother ran to the phone to talk to my father. "And she *got* it," I heard her say. "She went out and got it, all by herself. . . . Well, aren't you pleased! —Marjorie," she called. "Marjorie, come and talk to your father."

He was very pleased, as I knew he would be. Pleased, and astonished. "Do you think I had anything to do with swinging you in this direction?" he asked.

"I suspect so," I said. Because, perhaps, he had.

"Daddy, it may be that I just wanted to do something different," I added. I didn't want to sound too noble.

"There's nothing wrong with that, Marjorie. And I'm so delighted that—well, that you got what you went after!"

He was delighted that something good had happened to me for a change. I could also sense a certain amount of surprise in his voice. Well, no one was more surprised than I was.

"I'll have to figure up what you owe me," Bud was saying thoughtfully.

"Now, Bud, don't tease your sister," Mother said. "Good heavens, I should think you could let up on her a little now. But, Marjorie, you're soaking wet. Didn't you wear your rubbers! Get into something dry now."

Things were settling back to normal. Bud was teasing me, and Mother was worrying about my wet feet.

"I'll only be here weekends," I said, still staring at the paper. "I'll have travel expenses and be all over the state."

Maybe it would be a good thing. As long as I was here, Bud would tease me, Mother would worry, and Daddy would shake newspapers at me.

"Oh, dear," said Mother. "Oh, *no*. And yet, it will be good for you, really."

"You have to keep an expense account?" asked Bud, horrified. "This will be the final blow to the national economy."

I ignored him.

"I'll miss all this," I said, unexpectedly. I was aware, suddenly, that I would. I would miss the living room with its fireplace and the clutter of books and magazines; I would miss breakfasts on the glassed-in porch; I would miss my room, and the one bathtub upstairs, and even Abby's radio, squawking in the kitchen.

"I'll be back weekends," I repeated.

My mother was in a flurry about what I would need and what we must do right away, but I told her that all I really had to have were some sensible shoes. We went upstairs to see what I had in my closet. I did have one pair of shoes that would do, but the heels were badly worn because I had used them for years to walk to football games.

"I'll take those down to get new lifts put on them right now," I said efficiently.

"And I'll let you have my new reversible coat," Mother said. "It's plain, but it will be just the thing. Marjorie, you are going to do something so useful!"

"Yes." I tried not to sigh. I saw myself walking on forever, in sensible shoes and a plain coat, being useful.

My eye caught a gold-colored wool dress hanging on the curtain rod.

"Mother!"

"Oh—this. It was on sale, in a State Street store, and your size. I couldn't resist it. It will be just the thing to wear on a—oh, a dinner date, movies, something like that. You haven't had anything new in a long time."

"Mother, you ought to take it back," I said severely. I did not feel that I needed a gold wool dress. All I needed were sensible shoes.

"I can't take it back, and besides it will look well with your brown hat with the gold feather," Mother said somewhat illogically. "Are you going to take your shoes now, or wait until your father gets back with the Hudson?"

"I'll go now," I said. I was too excited to settle down anywhere anyway.

I borrowed the reversible, since it was still raining. Bud was sitting in front of the fire with a sheet of paper.

"I'm figuring out all the money you've borrowed from me since the second grade," he said. "Let's see. That comes to exactly ten thousand dollars and seventy-five cents, Margie."

"No!" I gasped.

"Bud, stop that right now," Mother said. "And don't call her *Margie*."

"Margie!" Bud called.

I said good-bye, and left.

Halfway down to State Street I felt rather hungry, and realized that, with all the excitement about the interview, I had missed lunch. I found two quarters in the zipper compartment of my purse; I would be able to stop at the State Street Drugstore. I started humming, slightly off key, dumped the shoes at the repair shop, and went to the drugstore. No longer did my clothes feel clammy or my hair straggly. I had a job; I was about to start a new phase of my life that would be better (how could it be worse?), and I had enough money for a milk shake and an olive-nut sandwich.

The sandwich, when it came, looked unusually good.

I had just started it when a voice said, "Do you eat those things even for breakfast?"

The voice was slightly familiar, but the tall young man taking off his hat, in front of me, was no one I knew.

"Why—hardly," I said, somewhat surprised.

"I just wondered," he said. "I was simply curious."

"How did you—"

Then I stopped and put down my sandwich. I did not have to ask him how he knew. Had this been a radio "serial," a shivery chord would have been struck at this moment—the sound of revelation—as I recognized the person looking at me. He had been the boy who had sat near me once, right in this drugstore, as I was eating an olive-nut sandwich and drinking a milk shake. (I had asked him if he wanted the catsup.) He was the boy who had stared at me one cold morning as I was walking with Charla, and he had wanted to meet me and had asked my brother if he could call me. We had joked on the phone about glamour girls. He was also the man who had stepped out of the dark and caught me as I slid along a sidewalk. The voice was the same.

"Take it easy, Bright Eyes."

I remembered the smell of cold on his coat. I

felt snowflakes melt on my eylashes. I heard my own laughter.

"Hello, Tom," I said.

"Hello, Margie."

He wasn't smiling. There was no friendliness in his face; everything about him was wary, taut, dismissing.

"Uh—sit down," I said. "Won't you?"

Of course he was wary. He had made a date with me, and I had broken it. I would have to get Bud to explain it to him . . . explain what? How could it be explained?

"Sit down," I said, again.

"No, thanks. I just stopped in here for some cigarettes. —Unusual, rain in February, isn't it?"

I was trying to swallow a piece of bread that had stuck in my throat. He was very good looking. I liked the force in his features; I liked the fact that his mouth, a very gentle-looking mouth, was set firmly in his face. I'd been look-ing for someone like Tom Kent for a long time. The boy dancing with another girl, at a party, had had this sort of face, until I met him. The boy I had dated the week before, at a party, and who was at that moment with another girl, had often appeared to have this kind of face; but that too had always proved an illusion.

I had waited a long time for Tom.

"I'd like to talk to you a minute—"

"I hope you enjoyed Hal Kemp, Margie."

He thought I had gone to Winter Prom.

"I didn't hear Hal Kemp."

"Oh?"

"I—" Surely I could explain. It was a *misunderstanding*. In the movies there were frequently misunderstandings between the Boy and the Girl, but everything was always cleared up for a happy ending.

"Nice to have seen you, Margie," Tom said, and turned away.

There was no way to explain. There was no way to clear things up. This was not a movie.

I put down my sandwich (among various things certain to me at the moment was the knowledge that I would never be able to eat an olive-nut sandwich again) . Rage, so fierce it was almost warming, filled me. It wasn't fair. It was simply not fair. I had been foolish to break the date for the Beaux Arts Ball, foolish to have let myself be influenced by Charla, foolish and wrong, but other girls got a second chance. Those dopey girls in the movies—*they* always got a second chance. Of course those movies were silly, but I could think of similiar situations that were not silly; Elizabeth, having a second chance with Darcy, despite his pride and her prejudice; and Kitty, I thought, angrily. Kitty had spelled out a message to Levin as they played a game at a party and they had gotten back together again. But none of that helped me; here I sat, in a drugstore, with a half-eaten sandwich, Cinderella among the ashes. I had met my Prince but I had lost him. That was the way it happened, in real life; if you were foolish, you did not get a second chance. No glass slipper would be left on a landing; no fairy godmother would appear and rescue you—nothing.

I sat there staring. There was no hope of help.

Tintern Witherspoon, wearing a velveteen

puddle on her head for a hat, brushed by me.

"You look terrible, Margie," she said. "You ought to get more sleep."

I pushed my milk shake away, got up, and started to walk to the front of the drugstore.

"Margie!"

It was Chucky Eaton. She came bursting through the door, shouting.

"I have looked all over for you; your mother said you were somewhere on State Street! Listen, we are having a party. Don got his Fellowship. We're going to England!"

Well, it was nice that someone was lucky. "I'm glad," I said.

"Anyway, we're having spaghetti—this weird recipe; it feeds a dozen on one pork chop, *unbelievable*. And we're having real wine. *Come*. At six. Bring someone, if you want to. Now, where can I find Jenny?"

"I can get a message to her," I said.

"Good. Oh, but I just had to find you; you've been so sweet to us, helping with Bump and all; my gosh, even staying with him the night of Winter Prom. —You will come?"

"Absolutely."

"Tell Jenny to bring Francis. —'Bye." She turned around and ran smack into Tom.

"Sorry," she said. "I really *hit* you, didn't I? Are you all right?"

"Oh—yes." Tom was looking very surprised. I had never thought that people could have round 'O's' for eyes when they were startled, but his were close to 'O's.'

"*Bring* someone, Margie," Chucky called back, and went out the door.

He stared at me.

"You didn't go to Winter Prom," he said.

"No. I didn't go."

Tom's face was now completely blank.

"You—took care of a friend's baby."

"Yes." We started out the door together, and then I remembered that I hadn't paid for my shake and sandwich, and went back and paid for them.

"I should have done that," he said, looking worried.

"Oh, no—you didn't need to, Tom.

We walked along the street. Neither of us

seemed to be able to say anything or to get started, somehow.

"About that 'explanation,' " he said, finally.

"I didn't go to the Winter Prom." I made my voice very definite. "I didn't go anywhere. I had decided—not to go anywhere for a while, for reasons that now seem too stupid to repeat."

"I—see."

"I stayed with Bump, the Eatons' baby, because they wanted to go out and didn't have anyone to leave the baby with." I paused. Something was still wrong. "Tom, I didn't break our date just to stay with the baby. I'd already broken our date. And breaking that date, I'd like to say right now, is the most unfortunate thing I have ever done."

We were walking along the street very slowly.

"I can't tell you how much I reget it and how sorry I am. The reasons—"

"You don't have to give me a reason," he said, helping me around a puddle. "You said you had decided not to go out for a while. Forget the reasons."

We looked at each other.

"By the way," he asked, "where are we going?"

"Where?" Oh, of course, he meant which way down the street.

"I have to stop by the School of Music," I said. "I have to leave a message for a friend, and the only way I can do this is to leave it with a boy she knows."

"All right." He took my elbow again as we went around another puddle.

"I liked the way you caught me that night," I said.

"You knew that was me?"

"I do now. Of course, I was silly to be sliding on the ice."

"You aren't the only one who has been silly. I should have believed your brother when he said that you were simply not going out, for a while. —Incidentally, I hope you're over that idea."

"I'm over it."

"Let's get it straight right now."

"Oh, I *am* over it," I said. I had something to get straight too. "Did you enjoy going out with Charla?"

"Charla." He sighed. "I thought her costume most appropriate."

I must remember to tell my father that.

We had come to the School of Music, and we went inside and up to the practice rooms. I paused outside one of the cubicles. Francis was in there, playing a concerto.

"He's pretty good," said Tom. "You aren't going to interrupt him, are you?"

"I would no more interrupt Francis in the middle of a concerto than I would walk in front of a train," I said.

I wrote a note and slipped it under the door. Francis called Jenny every afternoon; she'd get her message.

"He is good," Tom said again, as we walked through the rickety, old-school-desk-smelling building, past a door where a girl was screaming, "Ho ho ho *ho* ho ho ho."

"And those practice pianos are lousy, my mother says."

The concerto rose and cascaded behind us. Francis was indeed good, I thought; a lousy piano, a quarrelsome teacher—nothing could stop him.

"Ah ha ha *ha*—" screamed the girl. She was terrible.

"Did your mother go to school here?" I asked.

It seemed perfectly natural to ask Tom about his mother.

"Yes," he said, as we walked out into the rain. "She's very musical. My whole family are. But I'm not. I can't carry a tune."

"Ho ho ho *ho*—" I sang, to show him I couldn't do much better. I can't stay on key.

"Yes, but *listen*," he said soberly. "Ho ho ho ho ho ho *ho.*"

It was all one note. He was definitely worse.

"You can at least carry a tune," he said. "I can't even get a toe hold on one. Listen. —Ho ho ho ho."

I exploded with laughter.

"Ho!" I squeaked.

He took my arm and we went off through the rain, both "Ho-ho-ing." People turned to stare;

we stared back, singing louder, and collapsed in the doorway of U Hall, finally, gasping and shaking.

"Now, look," he said suddenly, seriously. "You're going to be around here, aren't you? You're not leaving or anything?"

"I have a job, but I'll be here weekends."

"That's fine. —What about tonight?"

"We'll go to the Eatons' party. She's the girl who ran into you in the drugstore."

It was perfectly natural to ask him to go to the Eatons' with me.

"Fine. Will you be here all week?"

"All week. Then I'll be gone until the next weekend."

"Good. There's a play we might want to see tomorrow night."

It was as though we had known each other for years.

"I thought," he said, "that day I saw you walking along in the snow, with that green thing jammed on your head, sort of squinting crossly into the sleet—I thought, *There's my girl.*"

"You did! I don't sound too attractive, squinting and all. —I was just cold. *I* thought, when you stepped out of the dark and caught me, that you were—well, that you were 'the one.' —I am much more romantic," I said.

"We're both romantic, Margie."

People pushed at us from the door, and we had to move; Tom said that he had better get me home so that I could get out of my wet things, and offered to call a taxi; but I told him that I was wet already and not to bother with a taxi and that if we cut through campus I would be nearly home anyway.

We cut through the campus.

I had never walked across the campus before and seen so many people who looked happy. Girls in trench coats and slickers were splashing through puddles; a giggling couple walked in front of us under the same raincoat; a Chinese girl, wearing a long slit dress the color of a flower, smiled as she passed.

"It almost feels like spring," he said. "You know we'll have more bad weather, but it feels like spring."

"Yes," I agreed.

I was thinking that, after all, winter did end. Quite suddenly, wherever you were, in a lead-gray lab or a classroom or back in the catacombs of the library's stacks, you would look up and smell lilac.

We went up my street and stopped at my door. We stood there half smiling, nearly laughing over nothing, when he suddenly released my arm and said:

"What if I hadn't gone into the State Street Drugstore today? What if you hadn't been there?"

He was not smiling now.

"Well, what if Chucky hadn't burst in at just that moment?" I asked. "What if she hadn't said just what she said?"

I was surprised at the intensity in my own voice. I had never talked that way before; I had always tried to say something to make a boy laugh. I had been afraid of any intensity, of sounding "boy crazy" or "fast," but I did not care how I sounded, now, and I was not afraid. According to my brother, I was doing what I was supposed to be doing. There was no reason to be afraid.

Tom told me to go in and get dry and warm and that he would call me, and then see me very soon.

We said "Good-bye," not smiling.

I walked slowly into the house and closed the door. I was glad that there was no one in sight. What had happened was almost more than I could bear, and I wanted to keep it to myself for awhile, to hold it, to try and believe it.

It was very hard to believe. I had been shaken by my ignorance, asked a question that required an answer, and, now, was touched by splendor.

Tom. He would call, soon, and then I would see him.

Abby's radio was playing a rather tinny sounding song in the kitchen; it squawked and stopped dead. A tune had also ended for me, but it was something I could never have kept, any more than I had been able to keep my corsages; and what was cascading around me now, filling me, lifting me, was music.

Date Due